BEARS DON' EAT EGG SANDWICHES

For Mum, who read me so many
crazy stories, and Dad, who made
up such fabulous ones. J.F.

For Owen Thomas. R.S.

Written by
Julie Fulton

Illustrated by
Rachel Suzanne

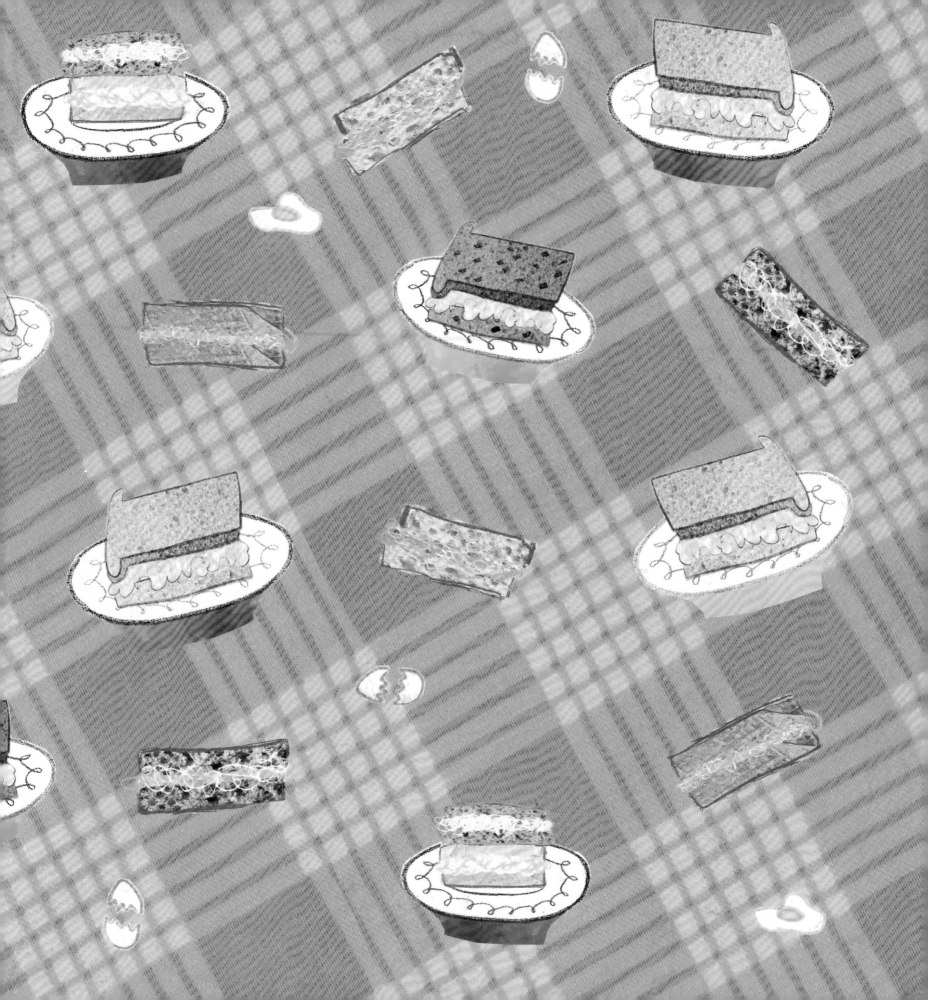

Jack was about to have lunch when

there was a knock at the door.

"Oh good," he said, "a visitor."

It was...

...a bear.

"I'm hungry," it said.

"Would you like an egg sandwich?" asked Jack.

"Bears don't eat egg sandwiches," said the bear.

"I love egg sandwiches," said Jack. "I'm going to eat one."

"I know what I want for my lunch," said the bear,

"but I need a big plate."

Jack found the biggest plate he could.

"Would you like an egg sandwich to put on it?" he asked.

"Certainly not," said the bear.

"I told you, **bears don't eat egg sandwiches.**"

"What will you put on it?" asked Jack.

The bear licked its lips with its long tongue.

"Something nice and tasty," it said.

"Egg sandwiches are tasty," said Jack.

"Have you forgotten already?" bawled the bear.

"Bears don't eat egg sandwiches!"

"I know what I want for my lunch," said the bear, "but I need a big spoon."

Jack found the biggest spoon he could.

"You can fit lots of egg sandwiches on this spoon," he said.

"Don't you ever listen?"

bellowed the bear.

"Bears don't eat egg sandwiches!"

"What are you going to eat?" asked Jack.

The bear patted its tummy
with its scritchy-scratchy claws.
"Lunch," it said.
"Egg sandwiches are good for lunch," said Jack.

"Enough of the egg sandwiches!" roared the bear.

"Bears don't eat egg sandwiches!"

"I'm going to have another one," said Jack.

"I know what I want for my lunch," said the bear,
"but I need you to sit on the plate."

Jack sat on the plate.

"Excuse me," he said, as the bear picked up the spoon.

"If bears don't eat egg sandwiches, what do they eat?"

"Well," said the bear,
leaning over Jack, "bears eat...

"But I'll taste of frog spawn and grass stains and snot," said Jack.

"No, you won't," snorted the bear. "You'll taste delicious!"

"I'll taste of dirty socks and bits of string and mud!" shouted Jack.

"No, you won't!" snarled the bear. "You'll taste absolutely delicious!"

"I'll taste of egg

sandwiches!"

yelled Jack, as he disappeared into
the bear's cavernous mouth.

The bear coughed.

The bear spluttered.

"Eeeeeuu

uuuuuucccccchhh!" it howled, as it spat Jack out.

"BEARS

DON'T EAT

EGG

SANDWICHES!"

"Shall I make you a cheese sandwich instead?" asked Jack.

The End

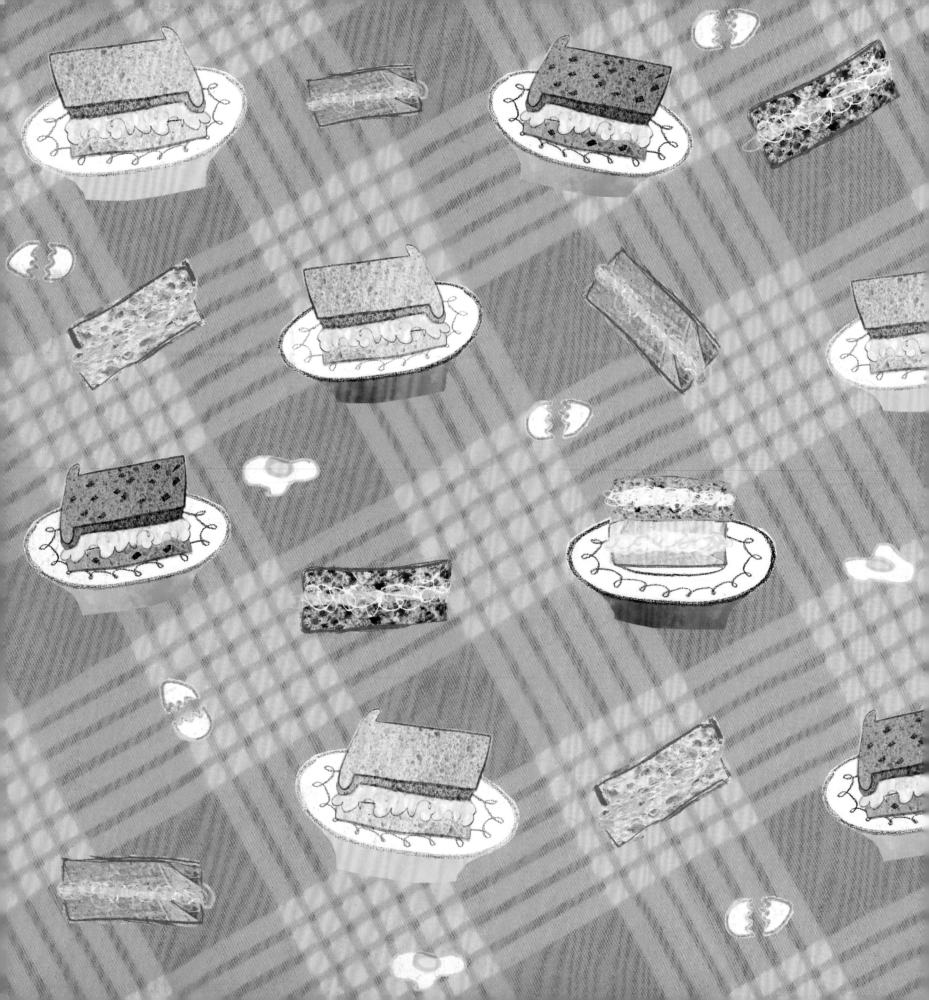

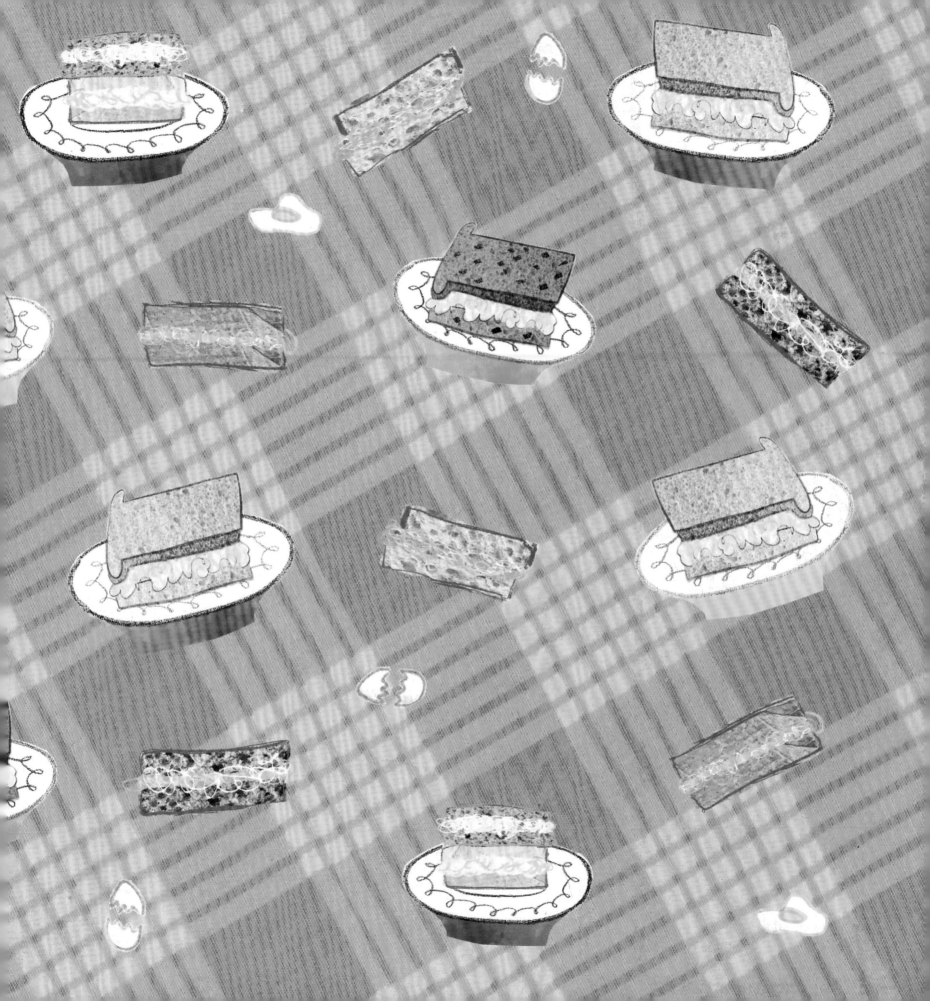

Bears Don't Eat Egg Sandwiches
An original concept by author Julie Fulton
© Julie Fulton
Illustrations © Rachel Suzanne, 2017

MAVERICK ARTS PUBLISHING LTD
Studio 3A, City Business Centre, 6 Brighton Road, Horsham,
West Sussex, RH13 5BB, +44 (0)1403 256941
© Maverick Arts Publishing Limited November 2017

A CIP catalogue record for this book
is available at the British Library.

Maverick
arts publishing
www.maverickbooks.co.uk

ISBN 978-1-84886-283-8